A Map of the County of

BARSETSHIRE

Shewing the Situations of the

various great Estates and Seats

HOGGLE END

HOGGLESTOCK

Rising Castle

WINTER OVERCOTES

Pomfret Madrigal

High Rising

SHEARING JUNCT.

River Rising

Low Rising

Little Misfit

Hatch End

Scannington

Boxer's Knob

Greshamsbury Hall

Pomfret Towers

Obelisk

Boxall Hill

Winter Underclose

EAST BARSETSHIRE

Ruddingdale

Lambton

Boxer's Priory

THE RIVER

Stogpingum

Eiderdown

Fleece

Worsted

Crabtree Canonicorum

Staple Park

Skeynes

Laverings Fm

Pookers Piece

Great Hump

Other books by Angela Thirkell

Three Houses (1931)

Ankle Deep (1933)

High Rising (1933)

Demon in the House, The (1934)

Wild Strawberries (1934)

O, These Men, These Men (1935)

August Folly (1936)

Coronation Summer (1937)

Summer Half (1937)

Pomfret Towers (1938)

Before Lunch (1939)

The Brandons (1939))

Cheerfulness Breaks In (1940)

Northbridge Rectory (1941)

Marling Hall (1942)

Growing Up (1943)

Headmistress, The (1944)

Miss Bunting (1945)

Peace Breaks Out (1946)

Private Enterprise (1947)

Love Among the Ruins (1948)

Old Bank House, The (1949)

County Chronicle (1950)

Duke's Daughter, The (1951)

Happy Returns (1952)

Jutland Cottage (1953)

What Did It Mean? (1954)

Enter Sir Robert (1955)

Never Too Late (1956)

Double Affair, A (1957)

Close Quarters (1958)

Love at All Ages (1959)